Number

Dorling Kinderlsey
www.dk.com

Editor Fiona Munro
Designer Lisa Hollis

Published in Great Britain in 1997
by Dorling Kindersley Limited, 9 Henrietta St, London WC2E 8PS
This edition published in 2000

A CIP catalogue record for this book is available from the British Library.

ISBN 0-7513-6701-X

Color reproduction by DOT Gradations
Printed in Hong Kong by Wing King Tong

Number One

COLIN AND JACQUI HAWKINS

Dorling Kindersley

Number One was the very first of all the Numberlies.

"I'm the first and so is my house," he said.
Number One lived in the first
house in Numbertown.
The address was 1, Number Lane.
"My house is the very best in
Numbertown," he said proudly.

Number One had one of everything
in his house. He had one bed,
one chair, one picture, one TV,

one table, one knife, one spoon, one fork,
one clock, and one book.

For one hour every morning, Number One rubbed and scrubbed everything in his little house until it sparkled.

At one o'clock exactly, he ate his lunch of one beefburger, one bean, and one big chip.

One day, after lunch, Number One looked around and said, "I need just one more thing to make my house perfect."

That afternoon, Number One waited at
the bus stop for one minute until
the Numbertown bus arrived.

"Room for one more," said the driver.
"One ticket to the pet shop, please,"
said Number One as the green bus
moved off down the road. Ding!
"This is my stop and here's the shop,"
said Number One, and he jumped off.

In the pet shop,
Number One
patted a big,
brown dog.
"Hello!" said
Number One.

"Woof!"

The dog gave one big,
booming bark. He was very noisy!

Number One said,

"Oh no! I can see
you're not the one for me."

Next, he picked up a fluffy, furry, fat cat.
"You're not noisy," said Number One.
The fat cat purred happily and
snuggled up to him.

Hello, puss!

"A-a-a-attishoo!"

Number One sneezed
an enormous sneeze.
The fat cat's fluffy fur
had tickled his nose.

Number One wheezed,

"Oh no! I can see
you're not the one for me."

Then Number One saw a brightly coloured parrot snoring and snoozing on its perch. It wasn't fluffy and it didn't look noisy. "Pretty Polly," said Number One. The parrot woke up and was very rude.

ZZZZ

"Clear off!"

it squawked. Number One cried,

"Oh no! I can see you're not the one for me."

"I'll never find the perfect pet," said Number One sadly as one big tear rolled down his cheek. Suddenly he heard . . .

Splish! Splash! Splosh!

There in a glass bowl was a fat goldfish.
It wasn't noisy, it wasn't fluffy,
and it wasn't rude.
It gave Number One a friendly, fishy smile.

Number One smiled, and said,

"Oh yes! I can see
you're **just** the one for me."

"I'll call you Goldie," said Number One
as they went home together. Goldie liked
the little yellow house. It looked
very sunny, just like Number One.

That night, Number One sang in the bath,

"You're the one for me!"

and Goldie smiled.

Then they watched television together,
and Number One sipped a cup of cocoa.

"I'm so sleepy," he said, and they
both yawned one enormous yawn.
"Goodnight, Goldie," said Number One.
One minute later they were both fast asleep.